# We Scream for Ice Cream

by Bernice Chardiet and Grace Maccarone
Illustrated by G. Brian Karas

**Hello Reader! — Level 3**

SCHOLASTIC INC.
New York  Toronto  London  Auckland  Sydney

The children in Ms. Darcy's class
were eager for the three o'clock bell to ring.

They could see the Rooty Tooty ice cream truck outside the window. *Ting-a-ling-ding-dong* went the truck, and *BUZZZZZZZ* went the bell.

The children raced to the ice cream truck.
Raymond Allen Tally got there first.
His initials spelled RAT,
and that's what the kids called him.
RAT's dog, Animal, always met him
after school.

Martin and Sammy followed RAT.
Then Bunny and Cynthia joined the line.
"Oh no!" said Bunny. "I forgot my money."
"Don't worry," Cynthia said. "I can lend
you some."

Brenda came along
with her little brother, Truman.
She pushed in front of Cynthia.

"This is a line," Cynthia said, "and I was here first."
Brenda and Truman had to go to the back.

"What are you getting?" Bunny asked.
"I'm getting a double chocolate ice cream bar,"
said Brenda. "If you get an ice cream stick
with a picture of Rooty Tooty on it,
it's a Lucky Stick. You win a free
ice cream sundae."

"I'm getting a strawberry cone," said Sammy.
"Don't get a cone," said Martin. "You can't
get a Lucky Stick with a cone."
"I don't care," said Sammy. "I want
a strawberry cone."

"Hey! Tell your ugly dog to stop sniffing my baby brother," Brenda said to RAT.

"I'm not a baby!" said Truman.

"Who are you calling ugly?" RAT said.

The Rooty Tooty lady called out,
"May I help someone? Who's first?"
"I am," RAT said. "I'll have a root beer float."

Martin got a Chocolate Nutty bar,
and Sammy got his strawberry cone.

Bunny asked for a Rooty Tooty Frooty bar.
She had never tasted one before,
but she liked the name.

"What can I get for you today?"
the Rooty Tooty lady asked Cynthia.
"I'll have a vanilla bar,"
Cynthia said. "No, that's boring.
I'll have a Frooty Coconut bar.
No. I might not like the coconut.
I'll have a Berry Tooty Nutty bar.
But berries make me itchy..."

"Hurry up," said Brenda.
"You're taking too much time.
Make up your mind."
"Oh, I'll have a rainbow ice,"
Cynthia said quickly.

After one lick, Cynthia knew
she had made a mistake.
She didn't like her rainbow ice
at all. Bunny didn't like her
Rooty Tooty Frooty
bar either.

Brenda was next. "I'll have
a double chocolate bar for myself
and a vanilla cup for my brother,"
said Brenda.

"I want ice cream on a stick,"
said Truman.
"No," said Brenda. "You'll
just spill it and make a mess.
Here. Take your cup."

"I don't want a cup," Truman shouted.
"I want ice cream on a stick!
I want ice cream on a stick!"
Truman threw his ice cream on the ground.

Cynthia picked up the cup and spoon.
She threw them in the litter basket.
"You shouldn't litter," Cynthia said.

Truman started to cry.
"I don't have any ice cream," he sobbed.
"You can have mine," said Bunny.

Truman sniffled.
"Thank you," he said.

Truman tried to make his
Rooty Tooty Frooty bar
last as long as possible.
But it was melting quickly.
"You have to eat faster," Brenda said.

"Okay," said Truman
and he took a big bite.
The Rooty Tooty Frooty ice cream
dropped onto the sidewalk.

"You made me do that!" Truman yelled.
He threw the ice cream stick at Brenda.
"I did not. You're just clumsy!"
Brenda yelled back.

Truman grabbed Brenda's arm,
and her ice cream fell, too.

Brenda looked down.
She saw something
on Truman's ice cream stick.
It was a picture of Rooty Tooty!
Truman had a Lucky Stick!

Brenda bent down and pretended
to tie her shoelace.
Quickly, she grabbed the Lucky Stick.

Bunny saw her do it.
"It's mine!" said Bunny.
"I bought it."

"No, it's mine," said Cynthia.
"You used my money."

"It's mine," said Truman.
"Bunny gave it to me!"

"Finders keepers, losers weepers,"
said Brenda. She waved the stick
in the air. "Now it's MINE!"

RAT was watching.
"Fetch!" he said to Animal.
Animal jumped up and grabbed the
Lucky Stick.
"Ha! Ha! My dog has the Lucky Stick,
so it's mine," said RAT.

"Good dog," RAT said to Animal.
"Give me the stick!"
But Animal ran away.
RAT ran after Animal and bumped into Martin.
The root beer flew out of RAT's hand.
It plopped to the ground.

"Let's get out of here," Sammy said to Martin.
"This is a dangerous place to eat ice cream."

Now, only Cynthia's rainbow ice
was left, but not for long.
"I hate rainbow ice," said Cynthia.
She let it drip and drip until
it was just a puddle on the sidewalk.

"What a mess," said Bunny.
"What a waste," said Brenda.
"We'd better clean it up," said Cynthia.
"Someone could slip on it and get hurt."
Truman and the girls cleaned up the mess.

"Look! RAT's coming back," Truman said.
"Do you have the Lucky Stick?" he asked.
"No," said RAT.

Truman cried louder than ever.
Everyone felt sad.

"I'm sorry," said Brenda.
"I shouldn't have been so greedy."
"I'm sorry, too," said Bunny.
"The Lucky Stick was really Truman's.
I gave it to him."

"Well, I still think I should have
gotten something," Cynthia said.
"No one would have had the stick
if I hadn't lent Bunny the money."
"So what?" said RAT. "All that means
is that Bunny owes you a dollar."

"I know what!" said Bunny. "I have some
Fruity Chewies at home. We can share them."

"I'll go home and get some cookies,"
said Cynthia. "My dad and I baked them."

"Then we can go to my house," said Brenda. "I'll share my swings."

Everybody had fun.
It was a good day after all.

And tomorrow, the ice cream truck
would come again, *ting-a-ling-ding-dong*,
down the street.